SANTA'S OBSESSION

EMMA BRAY

CHAPTER 1

Jenny

"*O*h my god, just go!" Eve scrunches up her pale, little nose as she tries to keep a straight face. I've been badgering my bestie with all sorts of questions about the hunk I dared her to kiss at the Halloween party a few months ago. He just so happened to be her new boss, but it took them a while to figure out who the other was because they'd both been masked at the masquerade. Theirs was like a super smexy fairytale story complete with the happy ending. They ended up getting married, and I'm truly happy for my best friend. If anyone deserves happiness, it's my dark-haired little friend Eve who was born on Halloween.

But I won't lie to myself and say that I'm not insanely jealous of her because I am. I've seen the way Eve's husband showers her with attention. He has eyes for no one but her, and I'm not stupid. I know guys like to look at me. I get hit on all the time, and I'm a shameless flirt, but it's all a front.

Despite all my talk, I'm still a virgin. I've just never found someone who makes me all gooey inside the way Lucian obviously does Eve.

I feel like a bit of a prude to be twenty-one and still a virgin. Maybe that's why I put on such a show with all my flirting—to hide the fact that I'm about as inexperienced as they come. All I've ever done is kiss. None of my friends would ever believe me if I told them I'd never gone all the way.

I just never could bring myself to give it up to some loser who I didn't feel anything for, though.

Maybe I'm too spoiled or too much of a romantic at heart, but I want fireworks. I want unbridled passion and to know that he's *the one* before I commit my body to someone.

Is that too much to ask?

"Jenny," Eve's amused voice breaks me from my reverie as she points out, "you're going to be late."

I glance down at my phone and jump up with a curse, "Shit! I gotta go! Love ya, girl!"

I give Eve an air kiss before I jump in my hot pink car. It was an early birthday slash Christmas present from my parents.

Yes, I love pink, and yes, I'm a Christmas baby. In the autumn, I'm an unapologetically pumpkin-spice loving, scarf and boot-wearing white girl. So, shoot me. I'm a walking cliche, but I don't care. I'm just me.

Whereas my bestie might have been born on All Hallows Eve, I was born on sweet baby Jesus' birthday.

My parents like to call me their Christmas miracle. They'd been trying for years to get pregnant before they were blessed with me, and then I came on Christmas like the present they'd always wanted.

Suffice it to say I'm an only child, and my parents dote on me. I love my mom and dad, and I've never been starved for affection or anything, but my parents are older, which means that they have some old-school ways of thinking too.

I huff as I high-tail it down to the mall, cursing traffic along the way. I'm cursing myself for getting too caught up and being irresponsible yet again. I always do this. Mom swears I'll be late to my own funeral, and I'm begrudgingly starting to think that she's right. It doesn't seem to matter how early I get dressed or how much I try to plan ahead. I'm always running late.

I try to reason with myself, though. It's not like I'll get fired or anything. This is charity work, something I volunteered for and that my parents think is a waste of time, but it's something I really want to do.

If my parents had their way, I'd never work a day in my life or do anything but sit around the mansion and look pretty.

But I get bored with nothing to do, and I love children. I think that's what I love the most about Christmas—all the happiness of children. Growing up without any brothers or sisters, I was often lonely and always wished I'd had another kid around to play with. Sure, Mom and Dad took me to their friends' houses, but all their kids were usually several years older than me, so I was kind of too little to really make lasting friendships with any of them. I was always the little tag-along kid who got in the way of what the older kids wanted to do.

Plus, I hate staying cooped in the house, and it's not like I need any more money or anything, so I volunteer down at the children's hospital as much as I can—another activity that my parents don't necessarily approve of, though they admit that it's an "admirable pastime."

They don't realize it's more than just a pastime for me, though. I want to make a difference, and I love seeing the kids' faces light up when they get a visitor, especially the ones who are only children like me and incredibly lonely. I play silly games with them and do whatever I can to cheer them up.

And I love every minute of it, even if it is heartbreaking to see them so sick.

The hospital is where I learned about this Christmas gig down at the mall. I'm all dressed up as an elf to be Santa's helper as kids sit on his lap and tell him all their Christmas wishes before getting their pictures taken with him. I'll be directing the line and giving out toys to every kid who shows up.

Though it was supposed to be a paying gig, I wanted to do it so bad, I made sure I got picked by promptly telling the hiring manager that I'd do it for free and that I'd donate toys to be passed out to all the kids.

His eyes had about bugged out of his head at my offer, and I'd been hired on the spot. No doubt he thought I was some special kind of crazy, but who cares, right? I'll be doing what I love and helping kids.

Of course, I didn't tell my parents where this was all happening at. I didn't exactly lie to them. I told them what I was doing. I just didn't disclose the location. They'd lose their shit if they knew I was working down at the mall, which they thought was in a dangerous location.

They worry too much, though. I'll be in a big building with tons of people about. It's Christmastime, and families will be shopping and bringing their kids by to get their photos taken with Santa.

It's going to be a blast.

Nick

I look down at the red suit lined with white fur in disgust. I can't believe I'm wearing this shit, but a job is a job, and they're scarce enough to come by for felons like me. I'm lucky as hell I was even hired to do this considering my felony status and how I'll be in close contact with kids.

Not that I was locked up for anything so heinous as harming children. My blood boils at just the thought of the type of scum that would do something like that.

No, I did time for protecting my dumb ass idiot of a brother. Him and all his hare-brained ideas of get-rich-quick-schemes. The ungrateful little brat hasn't even had the decency to show his face to me since I got locked up—much less since I've gotten out, and for good reason.

He knows I owe him an ass beating for the past two years I spent in prison for a crime he committed —not me. I swooped in to save the day and talk some sense into his fool head and got caught in the crossfire —as in I'm the one who took the fall for everything when the cops showed up and the shit hit the fan.

Sure, I could have saved my ass and ratted my brother out, but if there's one thing I learned from growing up in the Bronx, it's that you don't rat on anyone, especially family. Even if you get pegged for some shit you're innocent of, you keep your goddamned mouth shut.

It's a code I've been proud to live by all my life, and I still don't regret not breaking it. I might have lost two years of my life, but I still have my honor.

That doesn't mean I'm not holding one hell of a grudge, though.

And I suspect my little bro knows that if his continual absence and the fact that I haven't been able to locate him are any indication.

He's been living his life free and clear knowing damn well I've been sitting in a jail cell that had his name on it.

Now, I'm the one branded a felon, scraping by to

make ends meet, ostracized from society.

It probably doesn't help that I'm a big mother-fucker. I was big before I went into the pen, towering over most other men at six-foot-five, but now I'm bulky and rippling with muscles too. There really isn't shit else to do in the pen other than exercise, and I had to do something to keep myself from going crazy.

I put the itchy ass white, curly beard on and slap the damn Santa cap on my head, but that's as far as I'm going. I'm not stuffing this suit with stuffing to try to make myself look like some overweight, jolly fucker who eats too many cookies.

The man who hired me looks like he's about to protest when I fling the stuffing to the side, but one look at my glare and he wisely decides to keep his mouth shut.

"Your assistant should be here any minute," he says as he glances down at his watch with a frown.

I just nod, completely disinterested. I'd known there was going to have to be someone to play Santa's helper. I just wish she would show up so we can get this show on the road and I can get this day over with and cash my paycheck before I move on to the next gig.

I don't know why, but in my mind, I assumed it would be some middle-aged woman dressed up as an elf for this effort, some kindly woman who loved children and maybe was down on her luck and scraping by to make ends meet herself.

That's why when this bubbly, young bombshell comes rushing into the mall and over to where Dave, the hiring manager, and I are standing, I'm frozen still with shock.

Tall for a girl, her golden skin almost seems to glow with purity under the natural sunlight that's flooding in through the domed skylight of the mall. Her platinum blonde hair is long and stick straight, coming down to rest right down below her slender waist.

I swallow as my eyes sweep hungrily over the rest of her. She's wearing little red tights that leave nothing to the imagination and a short green elvish dress that shows off her subtle curves. A little elf hat is cocked prettily on the top of her head.

But what has my heart suddenly hammering too loudly in my head are the big green eyes that she turns up to me as she rushes over. They're green as emeralds and just as sparkling. She beams up at me, a full, perfect, white smile. "Hey, Santa! Sorry to keep you waiting. Ugh, I got stuck in traffic." She's a flurry of activity, talking animatedly while she gestures with her hands and smiles enthusiastically at Dave.

I feel a rush of completely insane jealousy rise up within me when she turns those eyes and that smile onto the other man. I only want her looking at me that way. A growl bubbles up in my throat. I'm confused and irritated by my reaction to this girl who doesn't look a day over eighteen. Fuck, she looks like she should be in line to sit on my knee and tell me what she wants for Christmas. You can bet your ass I'd do anything within my power to give it to her too. She might be dressed up like an elf, but she looks more like an angel sent down from heaven.

I feel my cock stiffen within my pants at that thought and take a deep breath to try to calm myself. For fuck's sake.

My eyes zone in on her ruby red lips that are glistening with gloss. They remind me of ripe cherries, and I just know if I tasted them, that's exactly what the fuck she would taste like.

"How old are you?" I bark at her, my voice coming out much more roughly than I intend it to.

Her eyes flick back up to me as a little furrow forms in her brow. "Um, twenty-one, but why does that matter to you, Santa?" She answers me sassily with a little toss of her head before she counters back at me, "How old are *you*?"

I'm only twenty-eight, but I don't tell her that. I

can't believe I'm only seven years older than her. I swear to God, the girl doesn't even look legal, but for some reason, I'm immensely relieved that she is.

"My name's Nick," I tell her. "Not fucking Santa." I can't stop the scowl that takes over my face. I meet the most beautiful creature I've ever laid eyes on and here I am wearing this ridiculous fucking Santa costume. I'm fuming with frustration and feel like an idiot.

A wide grin breaks across her face. "Really? Your name is really Nick, and you're playing Santa? Oh, this is priceless. Let me guess. Nick is short for Nicholas?"

I scowl at her. I realize she's making fun of me, but I'm so enamored by her smile, I don't even really give a shit. I'll let her laugh at me all day if it means I get to see that beautiful smile and that twinkle in her eyes.

I wipe the scowl off my face and feel my lips twitch. Her bright happiness and laugher are infectious. I could bask in her glow all day. "What's your name, doll?"

Do I imagine the blush that stains her pretty cheeks before she answers back with a cute little toss of her head? "Jenny."

"Jenny," I try her name out for size. "Short for Jennifer, I presume?" I ask her, raising an eyebrow of my own.

She frowns and fiddles with a piece of her hair as

she answers, "Well, yes, but no one calls me *Jennifer* except my mom, and that's only when I'm in trouble or something."

"Oh, I bet you're trouble, Jennifer," I tell her as I take a step toward her. Her scent, something like cinnamon and apples, teases my nostrils, and I feel my blood surging within my veins.

Her face colors and her breath hitches, but she stands her ground and looks up at me as she firmly corrects me, "Jenny." Then she goes on with a shrug, "Well, I'm certainly no saint." She looks back up at me with mischievous eyes. "Not like you, Saint Nick."

I love the teasing glint sparkling in her green depths. I could engage in this playful banter with her all day.

"Make no mistake, *Jennifer*," I stress every syllable of her name, loving the way it rolls off my tongue. "I am no saint. Far from it."

Before she has a chance to toss back what I'm sure would be another witty retort, Dave clears his throat beside us before announcing that we should get into position. The booth is set to open soon.

"After you," I gesture for her to walk ahead of me, now even more anxious for this day to be over with so we'll be off the clock and I can learn more about this little firecracker who's going to be my helper all day.

CHAPTER 2

Jenny

Good lord, this man is like no Santa I've ever seen before. He's tall and doesn't have the jolly old belly Santa is known for, though he still manages to fill out his red suit, just not in the traditional sense.

More like there's a slab of sexy all up in there. I just know that underneath that suit the man is pure muscle.

He's a mountain of a man. I'm not short by any means. At five-foot-eight, I'm no little fairy. I've often been told I was tall and thin enough to be a model if I wanted to do that—which I don't. Nothing against the girls who do. More power to them. I love playing dress up and shopping as much as the next girl, but the catwalk just isn't my thing. Never has been.

Back to this god in a Santa suit…I'm no shortie, but even I have to crane my neck up to look at him. It makes me feel small and petite, two things I've never really felt. For the first time, I think I'm getting a glimpse of how Eve must feel looking up at everyone.

I can't see many of his features clearly. He's hidden behind the suit and Santa's quintessential beard that I can tell is fake and isn't his real facial hair.

Yet, the way my breath instantly caught in my throat when I first saw him lets me know that underneath the disguise the man is insanely hot.

What I *can* see clearly are his eyes. They're a clear blue, like napalm pools. There is so much in his eyes that keep flicking back to me and resting on me throughout the day.

I'm never nervous, but this man has me all in a fluster. My skin feels flushed, my hands are shaking. I'm out of sorts.

And all because of the intensity I see in his eyes.

He looks at me like no one has ever looked at me before.

I can't pinpoint everything in his gaze, but I know

that it sends tingles of feminine awareness running up and down my spine.

I was a bit worried how he'd be with the kids, though. He was so growly and almost grouchy when we first met. But he's heart-meltingly great with them, smiling at each child and listening to their wishes with rapt attention as he holds them gently on his knee before posing with a picture of them.

As if I needed any more reason to be insanely attracted to him.

I'm not the only female who notices that Saint Nick is off the charts on the attractiveness scale either. I frown as I see all the giggling women in line eyeing Nick and practically swooning at his way with kids. I swear I've never seen such a long line to get pictures taken with Santa, and I know it's all due to Nick.

He catches me gazing at him again and winks at me, a twinkle in his eyes.

I feel a blush stain my cheeks as I look away and paste a bright smile on my face as I speak to the next child and begin leading her over to Nick to tell him all her Christmas wishes.

We go at it all day, and time flies by. I love talking to the children and seeing their bright eyes and happy smiles, but I also love the feeling of Nick's eyes on me all day, even if it does have me all in a tizzy.

At the end of the day, I'm burning with curiosity to see the real man behind the Santa suit. I can't keep myself from staring as Nick yanks the cap and head-piece off his head, followed by the fake Santa beard.

And sweet baby Jesus, is he gorgeous.

I almost faint from how breathtakingly beautiful the man is.

He has a dark brown beard that's neatly groomed and wavy brown hair that belongs on the cover of romance novels. It's not down to his shoulders or anything, but it's long on the top, and when he runs his fingers through it, ruffling it, my own fingers itch to do the same.

I watch as he unbuttons the long Santa coat and then shrugs out of it. He's wearing a plain white T-shirt underneath it, and I swear to God I can see every muscle in his chest and arms flexing with the movement.

The man is seriously ripped, looking like he's about to bust out of that poor white T-shirt at any moment.

He catches me staring at him and smirks before he starts walking over to me.

I raise my chin and throw at him saucily, "Aren't you a bit young to be playing Santa?"

I don't know how old he is, but I don't see a speck of gray in this man's beard or hairline, so he can't be much more than thirty, though he's definitely older than me. Something in his eyes speaks to his experience.

"You're dying to know how old I am, aren't you, princess?" he asks me with that teasing glint in his eyes.

I don't deny it. Instead, I just shrug and raise an eyebrow at him. "Well?"

He grins, flashing me a full, breathtaking male smile before he finally admits, "Twenty-eight."

"What got you into working the Santa gig?" I ask, truly curious as to why this man is doing this. Does he just love children like I do? He seemed grouchy about it at the beginning, which wouldn't make sense if he's doing this just for fun like I am.

He frowns but ends up not having to answer when Dave comes over and claps us both on the back.

"You guys were great!" He's beaming at us. "I don't think we've ever had so much success with a Santa booth before. We weren't even able to fit them all in! We've got a lot of people asking if they'll have a chance to get their turn tomorrow. So, what do you say? You two game for another round in the morning?"

I'm beaming, glad that it was such a success. Of course, I don't mind doing it again, but I glance over at Nick when I feel his eyes on me.

"I'll do it if *Jennifer* does," he says, stressing my full name, his eyes never leaving me.

My heart begins to thump harder in my chest.

"I'll do it if *Nicholas* does," I toss right back, stressing his full name. Two can play that game.

I watch as his eyes light up with humor.

Dave is oblivious. All he sees are dollar signs. "Great!" he announces as he claps us both on the back again before he asks me, "You still want to donate toys to each child and work for free? I'll understand if you don't since this was supposed to be a one-day thing, but I need to know."

His eyes are hopeful, and of course, I don't deny him. "Sure, no problem on both counts."

"Marvelous!" Dave is beaming as he walks away, no doubt feeling like he's gotten the best deal ever for the second time in a row, and I just smile.

I feel Nick's heavy stare on me and look over to find him regarding me thoughtfully.

"What?" I ask him with a half laugh to cover my sudden self-consciousness.

"You're doing this for free and donating free toys too? What are you? Some little rich girl?" he asks me with a laugh.

I feel my face burn at the way he says it like the

thought is ludicrous that a rich girl would be wasting her time on something like this.

I square my shoulders and level a look at him. "So what if I am? I love kids and want to make a difference."

His eyes widen when he realizes he's actually hit the nail right on the head with what he no doubt thought was a joke. "Damn, you really are a princess then," he comments, again studying me thoughtfully.

I feel my cheeks coloring again at the way he calls me "princess" and flick my hair over my shoulder to give myself something to do. What the hell is wrong with me? I've never been the shy, blushing type, but this man has me all up in knots.

"Well, see you tomorrow then, Saint Nick," I tell him, not knowing what else to say and suddenly ready to put some distance between myself and the effect this man has on me.

"Let me walk you to your car," he tells me as he comes to stand next to me, actually towering over me.

"Oh, that's okay," I tell him. "You don't have to do that."

"Oh, it's happening, princess, so don't even bother arguing," he tells me firmly but still with that twinkle in his eyes. "I can't let you walk out of here in that alone." His eyes trail up and down me, and suddenly my very innocent elf costume makes me feel indecent.

I swallow back a gasp before I collect myself and give him one of my indifferent shrugs as I begin walking away. "Whatever floats your boat, Saint Nick."

I hear him chuckle as he follows behind me and quickly matches my stride.

Dear God in heaven.

This man is going to be the death of me, and he hasn't even touched me.

Nick

I laugh out loud when I follow the beautiful blonde out to the parking lot and see her unlock a hot pink convertible with a fancy key fob. Oh, she's rich alright, and why does it not surprise me to see that she drives a hot pink convertible like she really is Barbie in the flesh? Not that she looks fake or plastic. It's not that by any means, but she has that perfect look about her with her blonde hair, emerald eyes, and killer figure.

She cuts her eyes at me. "What's so funny?"

"Nothing," I control my laughter but can't stop the grin that's spreading across my face. I finally sober, and my smile leaves my face when I realize this girl is way out of my league. She's probably an heiress or something whereas I'm a felon. She's doing this job as charity work just for fun, whereas I'm scraping by to get back on my feet and make ends meet.

We're from two different worlds.

I take the initiative to open her door for her and wait until she gets in before I close it softly behind her. "See you tomorrow, Jennifer."

"Until tomorrow, Nicholas," she bats my full name back at me, and I'm grinning again. God, she's fun. Full of wit and sass.

My heart drops down to my stomach. But, I'm a felon and she's a princess.

It could never work out.

My head might know that, but my body is another story. I dream of ruby red lips, long, blonde hair, and emerald eyes all night. I have her body clasped tightly to me as I drive into her over and over again, her green eyes sparkling up at me and her mouth open in a little "o" as she arches her back like a kitten and accepts everything I give her.

I wake up in a sweat, my cock hard as a rock. I lay

there, my chest heaving, visions of my dream dancing throughout my head.

Oh, fuck it. There's no way I can go back to sleep now, not without taking care of my erection.

I begin to stroke my length with my hand, a poor substitute for the body my cock desperately wishes it was in. I imagine how hot and tight her pussy would be wrapped around my pulsing staff, her arms wrapped around my neck. Oh Jesus, her pert little tits topped with nipples like berries, ripe for the sucking.

I increase my strokes. I haven't even been jacking off for two minutes, and I'm already going to come, the visions my mind conjures enough to send me quickly over the edge.

"Jenny!" I give a hoarse shout of her name as I grunt my release, thick, sticky ropes shooting up out of my engorged cock.

I lay there spent and limp afterward, frowning. My body might be momentarily sated, but I'm still restless and aching.

Beating off is only a temporary fix. It still doesn't take away this *need* for her.

I try to go back to sleep, but I can't. My head is still filled with images of green eyes and blonde hair.

And my fucking cock is getting hard again.

I glare down at the offending body part and then finally get out of bed to go clean myself up.

It's early as fuck. The sun isn't even up yet, but it's obvious I'm not going to be getting any more rest, so I throw on my jogging pants and hit the streets for a morning run.

Maybe exercising will help get my body and mind under control.

Because at the moment, all it's filled with is a certain little elvin princess, and I don't know what the fuck I'm going to do about it.

CHAPTER 3

Jenny

I didn't sleep well last night. Eyes like napalm pools, wavy hair that I itch to run my fingers through, and a sexy dark brown beard invade my dreams.

Nick.

I haven't been able to stop thinking about him. My cheeks feel all hot, and there's a pulsing between my legs that won't go away. I keep clenching my legs together to try to ease the ache, but it won't stop.

When I wake up from yet another tormented

dream of the man who's way too sexy to be playing a Santa Claus, my pussy feels wet and swollen. I let out a frustrated huff and let my hand trail down to the throbbing flesh between my legs.

I know women masturbate, but I've never been able to get myself off. It's embarrassing at my age, but I've never had an orgasm. I don't really know how to do it. I know you're supposed to pet your clit, and I've tried before, but I've just never been able to achieve that monumental rush of release that women talk about.

It's the same now. It feels good when I find that little bundle of nerves and press and rub on it, and I feel myself getting wetter, especially when I think about Nick. I feel a pressure building up inside of me, but I can't seem to get it to pop. It just builds and builds and then it recedes.

I let out a frustrated groan and fling my arm over my eyes before I finally give up and get up to take a shower.

It's still early, but I go ahead and get ready for the day ahead, taking even more care with my appearance than usual.

I'm never to anything early, but I'm actually on time for my "job" today.

My breath hitches in my throat when I walk into the mall and am hit with all his big gloriousness all over again.

He's already suited up in the red Santa pants, though he's only wearing a white shirt and not the coat yet. His wavy brown hair is stylishly disheveled, and his beard is just oh my god. He looks like such a *man.*

My stomach falls when I approach him and he turns those blue eyes to me, sweeping me quickly in his gaze before he turns away from me, obviously dismissing me.

My cheeks burn as I feel thoroughly rejected.

And that feeling only makes me want to lash out in anger.

"Nicholas," I greet him with a snooty tone to my voice. I almost wince. God, I sound like my mother.

"Jennifer," he nods back at me formally before he turns away from me again.

I'm suddenly seething. "It's Jenny," I remind him from behind clenched teeth.

He doesn't say anything. He ignores me completely, and I'm baffled. I'm not used to being ignored, and I don't know what's changed. I saw the way he was looking at me yesterday. I know I didn't imagine the appreciation in his eyes or the way he flirted with me.

So, what's different today?

Just then Dave shows up to put us out of our misery and break the awkward silence that's settled between us. If our "boss" notices the thick tension between us, he doesn't comment on it. He just reminds us to be ready to go in five, and then he's off.

I watch Nick out of the corner of my eyes as he shrugs on the Santa coat and then fits the fake white beard and hat onto his head.

Apparently, I must turn toward him and am watching him full on because when he looks up, our eyes meet.

I see his eyes flare with heat. He stares at me, his blues shining brightly, and my breath hitches in my throat. The intensity in his gaze is like nothing I've ever seen before. I could bask in it forever.

But then he turns away from me again, and I feel bereft, like a cloud has just rolled over the sun.

Our booth opens, and the children—and swooning mothers—begin rolling in. I smile at the children and try not to glare at the tittering women.

Something tells me today isn't going to be as fun as yesterday was.

Nick

It's both killing me and sustaining me to be in her presence. I can't stop myself from looking at her out of the corner of my eye, drinking in her essence, everything that is her. Yet, I'm trying my best not to look at her directly or have much contact with her. She's a rich girl, and I'm a felon, so there's no use in encouraging anything between us. Once she finds out what I really am, she'll run the other way so fast. And I couldn't blame her. No matter that I really am innocent of the crime I was charged with. I accepted the guilty verdict, and I did the time. I'm branded what I am.

There's no changing any of that.

But fucking hell does she look amazing. Every time she comes over to me, leading a child to me by the hand, I get a whiff of her scent. She smells warm and inviting like cinnamon and applies.

She smells fucking delectable, good enough to eat. And it's all I can do to keep from throwing her over my shoulder caveman style and marching her straight back to my apartment where I can spread her out and feast on her the way I want to. I want her legs on either side of my head while I'm nose deep in her pussy.

Fuck me.

I force those thoughts away, very aware of where we are and the children who've come to see Santa. I can't ruin their dreams with my frustrated attitude.

And fuck am I frustrated. I haven't been with a woman since before I went to prison. My hand has always been good enough for me. I can't remember the last time my body was teeming for a certain female.

Actually, yes, I can.

Never.

I've never needed a woman as badly as I need Jenny.

I don't know how I get through the day, but somehow I do. Again, there's a hoard of disappointed children and mothers who didn't get a chance for their picture with Santa, so I'm halfway optimistic that our gig will be extended another day.

Will Jenny do it again? It's torture thinking of spending another day in such close proximity to her, but it's also torture thinking of never seeing her again.

"I said 'no,' you creeps," Jenny's irritated voice floats over to me, and I swiftly turn to her once I register what she said.

The scene before me makes my vision go red. There are two young guys standing in front of her, lasciviously eyeing her in her little elf costume. "Aw, come on, baby. We've got a couple of toys you can play with," one says while elbowing his friend in the ribs.

The other one reaches out a hand to touch her, and that's when I surge forward like a bull after a red flag, grabbing his hand harshly and stopping its travel midway before he can touch her.

"Ow, what the fuck, Santa?" the little jerk whines up at me.

"Don't fucking touch her," my voice is deadly calm, but the little pricks must hear the clear warning in it because their eyes go wide before they wisely take a step back, holding up their hands. "Hey, we were just having some fun, man."

The insinuation that these two little idiots think it's fun to accost women only angers me again, and I take another step toward them, fulling intending to pummel them into the ground, but then I feel a tiny hand on my arm.

I still. It's the first time she's touched me, and even though we have layers of clothing between us, I feel that touch on my skin like a brand. Every cell in my body suddenly surges to life, and my blood begins pumping rapidly throughout my veins.

That touch detonates something inside me.

"Come on," I order her, my voice coming out more

gruffly than I intend it to as I close my hand around hers, the sensation of her skin meeting mine through our palms sending a jolt through me. I begin leading her to Dave's office.

She hurries to keep up with me as I pull her along. "Nick, what the fuck?" she whispers to me as I continue to pull her to my destination.

"Don't swear," I admonish her. She's too perfect to be swearing. She's an angel, and she shouldn't be tainted by anything—even foul language.

I'm relieved to find Dave's office empty, though it wouldn't have really mattered if it hadn't been. I'd have ordered the fucker out anyway, but this saves me time from pissing the old man off.

I yank Jenny inside and slam the door behind her, swiftly turning the lock to it.

"Nick, what the—?"

I don't even give her time to swear again.

In less that a second, I have her pressed up against the door, my body flush against hers. Sweet Jesus, does her body mold perfectly into mine.

I yank the fucking Santa cap and beard from my head, and then my lips are crashing down onto hers.

I was wrong. She doesn't taste like cherries. She tastes even better.

Cinnamon and apples. Like baked apple pie. How the fuck does she taste just like she smells? I growl as I feel her go pliant beneath me, her body melting against mine, and a surge of animalistic male pride sweeps through me at her submission.

Fuck, she wants this.

Her mouth opens easily when my tongue bids for entry, and then I'm tasting her, mating my tongue with hers, and I feel like I've come fucking home. Until this moment, I've been wandering, looking for something. I didn't even know I was lost until this moment when I become found.

Jenny tastes like *mine*.

Nothing in my fucked-up life has ever felt as right as this, and in this moment, I don't give a fuck about society or convention. I'm not even thinking about how she's lightyears out of my league.

All I'm thinking about is us. The way her body is pressing against mine. The way she practically purrs against me as she kisses me back sweetly.

I bend my knees and press my hardness between her thighs, showing her just how badly I need her.

She gasps into my mouth, and I swear to God, I can feel her wetness leaking through her panties and tights and my ridiculous red Santa pants. I'm going to have a big wet spot on the front of these pants, but I don't give a fuck. I'll wear her juices on my pants like a badge of honor.

When I finally pull back from her long enough to give us a moment to breathe, my head is spinning. "Fuck, I've been wanting to do that since the moment I first laid eyes on you," I tell her.

She gives a shaky laugh. "I thought you hated me this morning."

"Never," I place my forehead against hers and shake it gently. "You're all I've been able to think about. I'm fucking obsessed with you, princess."

"I thought of you too," she admits to me breathlessly, a pretty blush staining her cheeks.

I pull back to look down at her fully, my lips tilting up at the thought that she was thinking of me too. Then, I smirk when I realize what she's really admitting.

"Did you pet your little pussy while you thought of me, princess?" I ask her huskily, my cock swelling even more at the thought.

She nods shyly, and I feel a jet of cum of shoot from the tip of my cock, staining the insides of my boxers.

Fuck me. I've got to have her. Right now.

"Fucking hell," I groan before I take her lips again. My hands find the band of her tights and yank them and her panties down in one fell swoop before I quickly pull my cock out of my own pants.

I'm still kissing her, and she moans into my mouth when my I move my hand between us to gather some of her wetness. My fingers find her clit, rubbing gentle circles around it.

She whimpers into my mouth, and her arms tighten into bands around me.

I continue to rub circles around her little bundle of nerves until she finally breaks our kiss, throwing her head back and crying out.

Moisture floods my fingers. She's dripping fucking wet, and I'm leaking, ropes of precum dribbling onto the floor between us.

Her skin is flushed, her lips are red and swollen from our kisses, and I've never seen anything more beautiful in my entire life.

"Fuck, fuck, fuck," I chant as I quickly hoist her up in my arms, wrapping her legs around me. "I can't wait," I manage to grate out as I line myself up at her hole and jam my head inside her.

"Nick…" I faintly hear her calling my name, but I'm too far gone to register it until I've already thrust inside her hard and deep. She's so fucking tight I might actually pass out from pleasure. Fuck, she feels too good. Too good!

She screams, and I still when I realize what I felt give way under my penetration.

I pull out slightly, and she screams again at the friction as I look down between us and see the blood coating my cock.

Goddamn. She's a fucking virgin.

CHAPTER 4

$\mathcal{I}$'m screaming in pain at his sudden invasion. I didn't even get a chance to see Nick's cock before he jammed it up inside me, but I can tell by the stinging way I'm stretched that he's just as huge there as he is everywhere else.

"You're a virgin?" Nick's eyes are regarding me incredulously as he raises them up from between us where I'm sure he's seen his cock coated with blood.

"I'm sorry," I mumble, embarrassed beyond measure.

He lets out a choked laugh. "You're sorry? Princess, you have nothing to be sorry for. I'm the one who's sorry. Dammit," he curses himself. "I was too rough with you. I'm so fucking sorry, Jenny." My heart melts when he says my name. Not *Jennifer* but *Jenny*. It shows me he really is concerned about me.

He continues to curse himself, berating himself for taking me so roughly my first time. I feel him start to slide out, and I tighten my arms and legs around him, struggling to push myself down onto him more fully.

It doesn't hurt anymore, though it's not exactly comfortable.

Still, I want this. I want my first time to be with Nick. I want it to be good for him. I suddenly know with perfect clarity that there is no one else I'd want to give my virginity to than this man.

He groans as I continue to squirm on him before he finally pushes into me a little more and then hisses between his teeth.

When he pushes up into me, I let out a moan of pleasure at the delicious friction of him moving inside me. My nerve endings are crackling with tingles that settle deep inside me, and I want more.

"You like that, baby?" he whispers right against my mouth, his eyes studying me.

"Uhm-hmm," I moan again as he moves cautiously inside me.

I see the tendons standing out on his neck, and every muscle in his body seems to be tense. Sweat is breaking out on his forehead.

It's obviously taking him a great effort to hold himself back, and that knowledge fills me with a surge of feminine power.

I push myself down onto him and gasp as I feel him hit a spot deep inside me.

"Fucking hell," he groans out as he holds me there. "You're so fucking tight, baby. I don't know if I can go slow."

"Don't," I tell him, giving him permission to give us what we both need.

His eyes are burning into me. He looks torn with indecision. "You need it slow your first time, baby. I should have given you romance, flowers and shit, led you into it gently instead of popping your cherry like a goddamn savage."

I try to push myself down onto him again, but he's holding me firmly with his hands on my waist.

I let out a whimper of frustration as he continues to try to talk himself out of doing what he really wants to do.

"Nick!" I finally whine as I place my hands on either side of his face and look him directly in the eyes. "I want this," I try to reassure him.

When he continues to stare at me uncertainly, I finally half sob, "Fuck me! Please!"

I watch the change happen as his eyes suddenly

heat and darken with lust, and then the animal within him takes over as he finally starts to fulfill my request.

He holds me firmly against the wall as he pulls out and hammers back inside me.

I scream again but this time in pleasure and not in pain.

My eyes close of their own accord.

"Look at me baby," he tells me, and I melt again at the way he calls me "baby." My eyes snap open to obey him, and I'm assaulted by his intense, piercing blue orbs. They're burning with heat. "You okay?" he asks me on an exhale of breath.

"Yes," I moan. "Feels so good."

"Hot damn," he says before he slams back inside me.

I grip onto his big shoulders and hang on for dear life as he pistons in and out of me, faster and faster, the intense pressure within me building and building until I think I can't take it anymore.

His eyes are burning into mine the whole time, heightening the experience.

He growls, his neck straining again, and I feel him growing larger and even harder inside me.

It's too much.

"Come on me, baby," he puffs out as he continues to drive into me hard. "Cream all over my dick." That powerful thrust combined with his dirty words sends me tilting over the edge.

I shatter on a scream.

My first orgasm is nothing like I could have imagined. It's breathtakingly beautiful and I explode in a sea of white. I feel my muscles pulsing and contracting around that hard part of him, and then it feels like I'm floating, my arms and legs tingling and going lax against him.

"Oh fuck yeah," he grunts out. "That's what I'm talking about." His eyes are wild as he watches me come, and then he announces his own release with a shout of my name.

"Jenny!" he roars, and then I feel jets of liquid heat spurting up inside me. He holds himself deep while he continues to eject himself into me. It's so warm, and I feel full and sated.

He's still staring down into my eyes, his chest heaving, and then he leans down and kisses me again, this time sweetly, gently.

I'm in heaven.

Nick

I'm keeping her. There's no way in hell I can ever let her go now. Not now that she's mine.

Truly mine. *All* mine.

I'm the only man who's ever been inside her. I'm the only man who will ever be inside her. I feel like a wolf jealously guarding its mate.

No one will ever touch Jenny but me.

Fuck everything. Nothing else in this world matters but me and my princess.

Somehow, this beautiful blonde angel wants me too. I hold her against the door for a long time, reluctant to pull my cock out of her, but I eventually have to.

I'm still kicking myself for not being gentler with her on her first time, but she'd begged me to fuck her. I should have made love to her, but I already know it's going to be extremely hard to ever hold back with her. She brings out the beast in me. I can't think when I'm inside her. She's so tight, and with her emerald eyes looking up at me trustingly, I just go insane.

I've never felt such an intense connection with another person before. It's crazy, I know. We only just met, but I feel like she's the puzzle piece that's been missing from my life.

My girl is so bubbly and light. She's a representation of all the goodness in the world. I take her over to the food court and buy her a cinnamon bun and a coffee.

She has a bit of icing on the corner of her lips and rather than wipe it away, I lean forward to kiss her, licking the sweetness from her lips.

Her natural cinnamon and apples taste still tastes better than the damn cinnamon roll.

She kisses me back, and I'm sure other people in the mall are watching us, but I don't give a fuck. Let them eat their hearts out.

When I finally break the kiss, my eyes hooded and hers all dreamy looking, she breaks off a piece of the roll and feeds it to me.

I'm sure I look whipped to onlookers, but I let her press the bite into my mouth, gratefully taking it from her fingers like a pet dog lapping at its master's lap. I'll never deny this girl anything. Anything she wants me to do—no matter how ridiculous—I'll do.

I'm thoroughly and completely enchanted by her.

She's chattering away happily, and I swear it's never been so easy to talk to someone. I'm sure I'm smiling like a schoolboy with his first crush, but again I don't give a fuck.

I can't wipe the smile off my face. What man could when he has the attention of a girl like her?

Turns out my princess was born on Christmas, but that's not why it's her favorite holiday. She's an only child, and she loves children. Despite my probing questions, she doesn't talk much about her parents other than to say that they love her very much and she loves them. She looks away when she's talking about them, and my stomach sinks. I suspect she knows that her parents won't approve of her being with someone like me.

Someone who's not rich and in their social circle.

They'll shit bricks if they find out I'm a felon.

I've already gathered that she's a trust fund baby, and while that thought still makes me uncomfortable, like I'm not good enough for her, she reassures me every time her little hand brushes mine or she smiles at me.

I don't know what the fuck I've ever done to be able to deserve a girl like this, but I know that I'll never lose her. I'll do anything—anything—to keep her, and I swear to god I'll live my life trying my best to make her happy.

I know I need to tell her about my felon status, but I can't bring myself to say the words just yet. I'm terrified of seeing fear in her eyes or her saying she doesn't want to see me again if she finds out.

I don't know if I'll be able to accept that if she does.

I'm not exaggerating. I don't know if I'm physically capable of letting her go.

It about kills me when I close her safely up in her ridiculous little pink convertible, making sure she's properly buckled up, before watching her drive away.

And I know I shouldn't follow her, but I can't help it.

I do. I want to make sure she's gets home safely.

I keep a good distance behind her since I'm on my motorcycle, and she'd recognize me in a heartbeat if she happened to look back. I don't want to freak her out by following after her like a dog with its tongue hanging out.

I watch from across the street as she pulls into a huge, gated mansion. I watch as she gives the keys to her car to some valet who comes forward to park it for her.

She's beautiful. She's classy and well-bred. She looks so perfect amongst all the richness and finery of the place, and suddenly I'm filling inadequate again.

It doesn't matter how hard I work. I'll never be able to give her that. Would it be right of me to ask her to give all that up to be with me? The felon who's so down on his luck he's working Santa gigs at the mall just to make ends meet?

I should just walk away now before I make this

harder than it's going to be. My heart starts hammering hard in my chest at the thought of never seeing her again, never hearing her witty retorts or the way she throws my full name, Nicholas, back at me when I tease her by calling her Jennifer.

I don't fucking know if I can do it. I'm already in too deep. When I think about her moving on with another man, another man touching her, another man holding her, another man fucking her, my vision goes red.

I don't know how long I sit there propped on my bike, contemplating everything, but I straighten when a luxury vehicle that's not Jenny's begins coming out of the gates. I watch cautiously as the car pulls across the street over to where I've been sitting discreetly—or so I thought. Apparently not.

The back window of the vehicle rolls down, and then I'm met with a pair of emerald green eyes just like Jenny's, but they're in a male's face.

It's her father.

CHAPTER 5

Jenny

I drive to the mall the next day still floating on the cloud that is Nick. I can't wait to see him again. My mind played back the events of the day before all night long, the possessive way he'd protected me from those jerkoffs, the fierce way he'd claimed me, the sweet way he'd talked to me afterward in the food court, hanging onto every word I said.

I frown when I realize I didn't learn too much about him. He'd kept the conversation mostly on me. I make up my mind that I'm going to remedy that today. Today, I'm going to learn more about my Saint Nick. I smile at the nickname. He's my very own sexy Santa. I never thought I'd be one of those girls who had a Santa fetish, but if that Santa is Nick, then sweet baby Jesus, do I ever love a man in a red suit.

I practically bounce into the mall and over to our booth, but Nick's not there. I grin to myself to think that I'm finally the one on time and he's the one running late.

When he finally does show up, it's one minute before the booth is set to open, and he's already completely outfitted in his Santa costume with the beard and cap on.

"Hi!" I chirp at him excitedly.

He hardly spares me a glance as he answers back gruffly. "Hey."

My smile falters. What the fuck?

"Nick, what's wrong?" I ask him, concerned.

He doesn't spare me a glance this time. "Nothing," he says with his back turned.

He's lying. It's not nothing. He's done a complete one-eighty from the way he was last night. The Nick from the night before hadn't been able to keep his eyes or hands or lips off me.

This Nick can't bear to look at me.

Did I do something wrong? Did I do something to piss him off?

A feeling of hurt and humiliation washes over me when it hits me what's going on.

He's regretting what we did. He must have gone home and thought about how he didn't really want a girl who's so inexperienced. My cheeks burn. God, he must think I'm pathetic.

I want to crawl into a hole and die. I'm mortified. I consider just walking out of the mall and going home, but I see the children already lining up, and I'm torn. It wouldn't be fair to abandon them when I've committed to seeing this through.

So, I do what I'm best at.

I plaster a plastic smile on my face and fake it, acting like I'm still bubbly and happy and everything's fine and nothing can hurt me.

Even though inside my heart is breaking.

Nick

This is killing me. I hate seeing her like this. She's putting on a mask to cover how she's really feeling, and I feel even worse when I know I'm the reason she's feeling the way she is.

What kind of asshole am I? I had the most beautiful

girl in the world gracing me with the prettiest smile, excited to greet me, and I gruffly shot her down.

I mentally remind myself why I'm doing this, though.

Her father is right. I'll only drag her down with me. All Jenny has ever known is wealth and luxury. She might say she'll give it all up for me if she has to, but how will she feel when she's scraping by and struggling with a fuck-up like me?

If I really love her, I'll let her go—for her own good.

It's killing me that she thinks I'm a bastard, though, that she thinks I don't want her. I saw the truth in her eyes when I finally allowed myself to look into her emerald greens as she brought the first child up to me.

Since then, it's been *her* avoiding me, *her* studiously avoiding my gaze.

It's tearing me apart.

I don't know if I can take this. I'm about ready to say to hell with it and pull her into my arms right here and now in front of this mall full of people when there's a loud bang and people start screaming and scattering.

It takes me less than a second to realize what's going down, and I'm on Jenny in a flash, crashing her body down onto the ground and covering it with my own to protect her.

As I cover her with my body, my eyes scan the madness until I see someone who causes my blood to run cold in my veins.

My brother.

And he's the fucker holding the gun.

"Jenny, stay right here and don't fucking move. Do you understand me?" My voice is harsh, but I can't help it. I'm strangled by fear. Not for me, but for her. My brother has seen me trying to protect her, so he knows she's important to me, and if the fucker is crazy enough to shoot up a mall to try to take me out, then he's definitely crazy enough to try to use my weakness against me.

"Do you have your phone, baby?" I ask her more gently.

She shakes her head, and I reach into my pocket and then press mine into her hand. "Stay here on the ground and call your father. Tell him where you're at, and ask him to come get you."

She whimpers as I begin to lift myself off her. I instinctively soothe her. "I want you to get up and run when I tell you to. You got that, baby?"

"Yes," she says, her body still trembling on the ground.

I stand slowly and hold my hands up in surrender as I begin walking over to my brother.

He's got the gun trained right on me. People are still scattering, though some have stopped in shock and have their phones out to record the scene playing before them. Idiots! They need to just get out of here.

I don't say anything to them, though. My sole focus is on my brother and keeping his attention on me so he doesn't harm Jenny.

"Long time, no see, brother," I greet him sardonically.

His eyes are wild-looking, and he runs a shaky hand through his hair.

"Put the gun down, Chris," I urge him evenly. "We can talk about all this like brothers."

"No, you'll kill me," he says, his voice shaking as much as the gun in his hands.

My eyes widen. Does he really think that? Is that what this is? He's trying to take me out before I take him out?

Sure, I owe him an ass-beating, but kill him? He's my brother. My stomach drops when I realize just how far down my brother has gone. He's really become unhinged.

"Why would I do that, Chris?" I ask him calmly.

"You know why!" he shouts at me. "You took the fall for me. You had all those years in prison to plot your revenge. I'm not stupid, Nick!"

"I took the fall for you," I emphasize to him, taking another slow step toward him. "I let them take me when you were the one who was guilty. Why would I do that if I was going to kill you? I was protecting you, you bonehead, like I've always done ever since we were kids. That's what big brothers do, right?"

He looks so much like the little brother I used to know when his bottom lip trembles and tears glisten in his eyes. "I've really fucked up this time, Nick," he says, as if it's finally hitting him just what he's done.

Yeah, he has. He's just shot up a mall, and I pray to God no one was injured or killed. "We'll fix it," I try to soothe him. "Just put the gun down, Chris."

He hesitates. He's considering doing it. I've almost got him. I'm just one step away from getting the gun from his grasp.

Out of the corner of my eye, I see police officers with their guns drawn creeping up on either side of my brother.

No! My mind screams. I want to yell at them to stop, to tell them that I've got this. He's my brother, and I can talk him down.

I never get that chance, though, because Chris moves his arm just the slightest bit, and a blast sounds.

I watch as the life drains instantly from my brother's eyes and he falls to the floor in a deadening heap.

CHAPTER 6

Jenny

The shooting at the mall is all over the news, the headline reading *Felon Santa's Brother Shoots Up the Mall.*

Nick is a felon. It suddenly makes sense why he was working the Santa gig. It was probably one of the only jobs he could get. I've watched all the videos people have already posted online. The one good thing that came out of all the onlookers recording everything was that Nick was exonerated. His brother admitted that he'd actually been the one guilty of the crime Nick had gone to prison for, and my heart clenches within me to think of Nick rotting away in prison for years for a crime he didn't commit.

It's been two days since the shooting. Two days since my distraught father showed up to rescue me from the site of the shooting, looking down his nose in distaste at everyone in the shopping complex before casting accusing eyes at me.

I'd shrunk in on myself. I'd known they wouldn't like me working there, but I'd done it anyway. I don't regret it. I did good work. I thought of all the kids I'd made happy with the free gifts.

I think of how I met Nick there. I wouldn't trade meeting Nick for anything.

I haven't seen or spoken to him since he was pressed on my back, shielding me from danger.

He's stayed away from me. I've tried to call his phone number, but he won't pick up.

I'd thought when he was so gruff with me that day that maybe he'd decided he didn't want me, but when mayhem had broken out, he'd instantly flown to protect me.

Would he do that if he didn't care about me?

I remember the way he'd called me "baby" and how gently he'd spoken to me, trying to calm me down when I was so frightened I was about to pee my pants.

But maybe that was just him trying to soothe a scared girl. Maybe it didn't mean anything.

No, I can't believe that. I don't know what happened between the day he'd taken my virginity and the day of the mall shooting, but I know I didn't imagine the intensity and adoration in Nick's eyes. I don't know much about sex, but I *know* that hadn't just been sex.

What we have is so much more meaningful than just sex. The way he'd insisted I look at him, the way he'd held my gaze the entire time we'd been moving together, our hearts beating as one.

My mother is sitting on the couch next to my father squeezing his hand tight as we all watch the news together. She's been beside herself since her daughter's near-brush with death, and while I'm never a prisoner here—I'm certainly old enough to come and go as I please—I've confined myself to staying close to her so as not to worry her anymore. For the past two days, she keeps seeking me out to stroke my hair and whimper pitifully over me, bemoaning how she could have lost me.

I love my mother, but you'd think *she* was the one who'd been in the shooting the way she's been carrying on. I've tried to assure her I'm fine, but she's still all worked up about it.

"We just knew something like this was going to happen," she wails.

My father shoots her a warning look, and I hone in on what she said, sitting up straighter in my chair.

"What do you mean you knew something like this would happen?" I question her, my heart suddenly beating overtime in my chest.

My father curses under his breath and then pinches between his brows. "Dad, what is she talking about?" I look to my father for answers.

Everything suddenly begins to click. All of my supposed freedom and independence was all an illusion. They've known everything all along. "Have you been having me followed?" I ask incredulously.

Dad shoots a withering glare at my mother for spilling the beans, but she doesn't pay him any mind. She's still distraught, her tearful eyes on the TV screen.

"It was for your protection, honey," Dad says. "We weren't trying to control you or anything. We just wanted to make sure you were safe."

The cogs are still turning in my mind as something else clicks into place. "Nick," I whisper.

I see my father wince, and I already know the answer before I ask the question.

"You talked to Nick?"

Suddenly it all makes sense. The reason Nick was

so distant the day after we'd had sex. We'd been sitting in perfect view of everyone in the food court. If my parents were having me followed, they'd no doubt heard about that.

And my father had immediately tried to put a stop to it.

"What did you say to him?" My voice is glacial. It almost gives me pause. I've never spoken to either of my parents in such a tone before, but I can't help it. I'm livid at the thought that my father interfered with my relationship with Nick.

He seems taken aback by my tone as well. He blinks before he states calmly, "Nothing that he didn't already know, dear."

My heart is wrenching within me. Poor Nick! I can just imagine what my father said to him, the way he probably talked to him in his high-handed manner, warning him away from me, telling him that he's not good enough for me.

Nick hasn't been ignoring me because he doesn't want me.

He's been doing it because he wants what's best for me. He truly loves me.

I feel tears prick my eyes as I burst out, "I love him!"

My mother's head snaps up, and my father's eyes

narrow at my outburst.

"Jennifer," my mother begins softly, pleadingly, "think about what you're saying. You can't possibly have a life with this man. He's a felon for God's sake."

"No, he's not," I instantly rush to his defense, "or haven't you been comprehending what you've been watching on the news? He's been exonerated. He's innocent. He did time for a crime he didn't commit, all to protect his brother." If anything, that spoke of a deeply rooted honor my parents couldn't even comprehend.

My heart is suddenly near to bursting with love for Nick, and I jump up from my chair.

My father stands with me, eyeing me warily. "Where are you going, Jenny?"

"Where does Nick live?" I ask him.

His eyes fall, and his lips press into a thin line.

"I know you know, Dad. If you had him investigated, you know. I'll find him with or without your help. It would be safer if I had your help, though," I point out, playing the safety card, hoping that will get him to 'fess up.

It does. When he takes in the stubborn set to my jaw, he realizes it's useless to try to stop me.

He still tries again, "We wanted so much more for you, Jenny."

I soften. I know my parents love me. I know they only want what's best for me. "Do you love Mom?" I ask him.

"More than anything," he answers immediately as he takes her hand, almost instinctively.

"Would you still love her if she was poor? Would you still want to be with her?"

My parents share a look. My mom's face is suddenly tender and full of sympathy, and my dad's is filled with defeat. His shoulders slump. He knows he's lost.

He tells me Nick's address, and I fly out of the house.

Nick

I feel like all the light has been snuffed out of my life. I should be celebrating. I've been exonerated. The governor issued me an official pardon already. I'm no longer considered a felon. I have my life back.

Except that it means nothing without my little elf. Without Jenny.

I've sat here in my apartment all alone for the past two days. I got drunk the first. I just sat here morose the second, replaying every memory I have of her. I know her father's right. I'm not good enough for her, and I never will be—felony status gone aside. I'm still not enough for her. I'm not rich. I'm not well-bred.

I'm still a street rat.

I've been mourning the loss of my brother too, though truth be told I think I lost my brother a long time ago. I don't know what happened to make him snap, but he turned into someone I didn't recognize years ago.

I don't know what I'm going to do. Everything inside me is telling me to go get my girl, but I have to do what's best for her. Isn't that real love? Sacrificing what you want most for the good of the person you love?

I saw Jenny's missed calls, and while it killed me not to answer her when she was calling for me, I couldn't bear to hear her telling me she never wanted to see me again because I know that's what she was going to say. She'd probably chew me a new one for lying to her, for not telling her upfront who she let take her virginity.

I can't be sorry about that, though. In my mind she's still mine. I don't know how the fuck I'll bear it if she moves on and starts dating other men—and she will because Jenny is too beautiful to be alone. I'll probably put a bullet straight through my fucking head to put me out of my misery.

Suddenly, there's frantic knocking at my door, and I scowl to myself, not knowing who would be here to interrupt my brooding. No one ever visits me. It's probably some neighbor wanting to borrow a cup of sugar or some fucking shit I'm not in the mood for.

I ignore the knocking, but it becomes more insistent.

I curse and stomp over to swing open the door, ready to tell whoever it is to go straight to hell, but then I stop, all the breath leaving my chest when I see who it is.

Jenny.

She's standing there in my doorway, every lean little inch of her, her straight blonde hair flowing down to her waist, her emerald green eyes looking up at me. Her cinnamon and apples scent is already enveloping me, and my eyes are drawn to her lips. They're not painted ruby red today. They're her natural puffy pink.

She's beautiful, and all I can do is stand there and drink her in.

Her angry voice breaks into my reverie. "I know

what the fuck you're doing, Nicholas, and it's completely unacceptable."

My eyes widen as I stare down at her. "What the fuck are you talking about?" How does she know where I live? Did she really come all the way over here to give me a tongue thrashing?

"I spoke to my father, and he finally confessed everything. You're staying away from me because you think you're not good enough for me." Her eyes are glistening with tears now, and her lips are trembling.

A tear escapes and begins making a trail down her cheek, and my chest tightens. I reach out to wipe it away. "Don't cry, baby," I plead with her. I can't stand to see her cry. I want her to be her happy, bubbly, carefree self.

"I won't if you don't make me!" she wails before she flings herself into my arms.

I wrap my arms around her and hold her tightly to me, my body finally settling now that she's back in my arms. Fuck, she feels so right. I don't know if I can do this.

"Jenny, you're father's right. I'll never be good enough for you," I try to make her see reason even as I tighten my arms around her, pulling her even closer to me, my body in contradiction with my words.

She ignores me as she pulls back just enough to look up into my eyes, "I love you, Nick."

I go completely still, and I can hear my heart beating in my ears as I stare down into her gorgeous green eyes.

They're shining with the truth. Somehow, against all odds, this gorgeous girl loves me. I could die right now and be a happy man.

I continue to stare down at her, warring with myself. I told myself I was staying away from her for her own good, but she came back to me. She's crying without me. She's not happy without me. I'm fucking miserable and downright suicidal without her.

I'm not doing anything but making us both miserable, so to hell with it.

"Fuck it, you're mine," I tell her as I cup her face with both hands and stare directly into her eyes. "I love you so fucking much, Jenny. I'd do any fucking thing for you. Even give you up if you wanted me to, though I think it would fucking kill me." My voice sounds as broken as that thought makes me feel.

Ever the little imp, she knows how to lighten things up and make me laugh. Her smile is mischievous, and her eyes are twinkling teasingly when she says, "That's a lot of swearing for someone who's supposed to be a saint, *Saint Nick*."

I throw my head back and laugh. God, I've missed her and her smart mouth. I was a fool to think I'd ever really be able to live without her.

"Yes, *Jennifer*," I tease her back when I've finally got myself under control.

"It's Jenny, *Nicholas*," she pouts prettily.

And then I kiss her, unable to keep from tasting her any longer.

"I'm fucking obsessed with you. You know that? I want to worship every fucking inch of you," I say in between nibbling on her lips.

"Then, do it," she mewls back at me.

And who am I to deny her anything?

Three Years Later

Jenny

"Daddy, does Santa come down the chimney?" Noelle, our three-year-old daughter asks Nick. Yes, we named her Noelle, a tribute to the holiday that brought us together. It might be a bit cheesy, but we are who we are. He grins and shoots me a look filled with innuendo as he answers her, "Yes, babygirl, he does."

I grin back at him, my body already heating at his words. We're already three years into our marriage, but we're just as hot for each other as ever—if not more so.

Nick didn't wait around after I showed up at his apartment to declare my love for him that day. We got married just a short month later, much to my mother's distress. She didn't have time to plan as big of a wedding as she'd wished, but she's lucky she got that. Nick had wanted to marry me the next day. He'd been generous to agree to wait a month to placate my mother.

Had it been up to Nick and me, we'd have been fine with a small ceremony, but in a gesture of goodwill, we'd agreed to let my parents throw us a semi-lavish affair.

I was grateful that my parents had seemed to come around after they saw how happy Nick made me. I think they could tell we're truly in love and that Nick would do anything to make me happy.

I think Nick's willingness to give me up because he thought it would be the best thing for me elevated him in my father's eyes. It still boggles my mind how well Nick and my father get along—so much so that my dad brought Nick on to work for him at his company. Of course, the fact that he wanted Nick to have a great salary so that he could properly provide for his daughter and granddaughter probably factored into his hiring decision, but I'm just happy that Nick seems to genuinely enjoy working for my dad. It wouldn't have mattered to me how much money Nick made. I'd be happy just being with him no matter what, and that's the honest to god truth.

Nick and Dad often sit in Dad's study playing chess or cards together while having a few drinks and talking. And Nick thoroughly charmed my mother just like he does every woman he's around. His good lucks coupled with his genuine manner gets women every time.

But he's mine. All mine. And he doesn't hesitate to let other women know it either. He only has eyes for me no matter where we go or how many women are throwing themselves at him.

I take care of our daughter while Nick works, but I also run a small preschool out of our home, so Noelle has plenty of other children to play with. She's still an only child for now, but Nick is trying his best to change that situation with how often he fucks me.

And good lord does he fuck me. He still mostly takes me hard and fast, just how I love it, but he's also started taking me slower too, making love to me until our release crashes over us like waves.

I love it however he takes me. I just love him, and I'll take him however I can get him.

Nick is my soulmate, and I can't imagine life without him.

He finally gets Noelle talked into going to sleep after he informs her that Santa won't come and deliver all her presents unless she's fast asleep. Of course, she wanted to stay awake to try to see him, but that statement from Nick made her eyes go wide before she comically pressed them shut tightly and tried to will herself to hurry up and fall asleep.

In the end, it was us sitting in her bed with her while we read her a Christmas story that did it.

We slip quietly out of our daughter's room, and then Nick bends down and scoops me up into his arms to carry me to our room, his eyes twinkling down at me the whole time.

"What do you think you're doing?" I ask him teasingly. "Santa's not off the job yet. He has to deliver a shit ton of presents to the living room so a little girl won't be disappointed in the morning."

"Oh, he's got time to do that," he assures me as he carries me into our room and then kicks our door closed behind us. "Right now, he wants *his* Christmas present."

He lays me on the bed and then makes quick work of removing my red robe and nightie. "Fucking hell, Jenny. How do you get more beautiful every day?" His eyes are filled with adoration as he takes in my body, and then he falls onto my breasts, licking and sucking them until I arch up with pleasure, my fingers finding their way to his hair.

My body is instantly on fire. He controls me with every touch, fanning the flames as high as he wants. He knows exactly how to touch me to make me lose my mind. Hell, he knows my body better than I do.

He kisses me everywhere, his hot lips leaving trails all over my stomach and thighs until he settles at the juncture between my legs.

I whimper, knowing what's coming. I can hardly take it when Nick eats my pussy. It feels too fucking good, and I usually come in less than a minute under his expert ministrations.

This time is no different. He has me screaming in thirty seconds flat, and then I lay there panting as he licks up the cream between my legs softly like a contented panther.

"Your turn, Santa," I tell him breathlessly when I finally get my breath back enough to get up and push him down onto the bed.

He falls back willingly and hooks his hands behind his head so he can look down at me where I'm kneeling between his legs.

I don't waste time teasing him. A long stream of

cum is leaking from the tip of his swollen cock and traveling down the side of it, and I lick my lips in anticipation.

"Jesus!" he shouts, his hips bucking up as I close my lips around him and immediately deep throat him.

Oh yes, I know how to make him nut in thirty seconds flat too. Two can play that game.

His hands fist in my hair as I continue to bob up and down on him, swirling my tongue around his tip when I come back to the top.

He's mumbling incoherent nonsense, and it fills me with a sense of triumph to know that I make him lose control like this.

I can feel him getting harder in my mouth. The tip of his cock is swelling, and he's fixing to come. I moan around him, ready to accept him into my throat, but then he pulls my head off of him.

I release him with a wet pop and a whine, feeling like I've been cheated, but he shushes me as he pulls me up to straddle him. He locks his lips onto mine as he thrusts up into me.

We groan into each other's mouths, and then he's fucking me just how I like it. Hard and fast, his big cock stretching me deliciously.

"Oh fuck, Jenny," he grunts as he continues to slam up into me, his hands holding my hips in place. He's pounding me so deep and fast, I can't do anything but let him hold me there and take it. "You want another baby, honey?"

I moan. He knows I do.

"You want me to breed you?" I feel the first spasms of my orgasm crash over me at his filthy talk. He knows I love it when he talks dirty like that.

"Get ready, baby," he growls. "I'm fixing to fill you up."

That does it. I spiral over the edge, screaming out his name. "Nick!"

His cry joins mine as I feel him stiffen right before his hot cum splashes up into me, soaking my womb. He holds himself in me deep, shooting his seed as far as it will go.

He comes and comes and comes until it's overflowing, leaking out around us onto my thighs and his balls. We're deliciously sticky, but he refuses to pull out, wanting to keep us connected for as long as possible. Nick always likes to stay inside me for a while after coming, and I honestly love it.

He gives a few more leisurely thrusts, and I feel more liquid spill out of him and into me.

I lean down to kiss him lazily, and he meets the languid pace of my tongue. God, I love him.

He rolls me over onto my back, his cock still deep

inside me. "Happy birthday, my love," he says as he strokes my hair back from my face.

"Merry Christmas, Santa," I tell him cheekily as I run my fingers along his face, feeling the softness of his dark brown beard.

He chuckles. "Best Christmas gift I ever got."

THE END

Connect with Emma!

Visit Emma's website to get a FREE book you can't get anywhere else: www.authoremmabray.com.